PARTY GIRL

EBONY Q.

THIS IS FICTION

ACKNOWLEDGMENTS

I thank you Lord for blessing me with this creativity and the courage to share it.

I am thankful for my family and friends for your love, support and encouragement.

I'm sending a huge thanks to my beta readers Divine, Dennis, Michelle and Karee for your time, input and support.

Thank you to my muse, Kaneka, for our daily conversations.

Thanks readers for giving your time to explore my work of art.

Last but not least, I thank my husband and son for going on this journey with me.

Thank you all so much.

Ebony

PERSONAL NOTE

Hey Ebony Q. Reader,
This would be impossible without readers like you supporting my dream. I'm crazy enough to go after what I want. Thanks for joining my journey. Ready to enter the mind of Author Ebony Q.?

Ebony Q.

CONTENTS

PLAYLIST

SONGS THAT INSPIRED THE CHARACTERS &
STORY

I Need a Hot Girl by Hot Boys (feat. Big Tymers)
Sho'Nuff by 8Ball & MJG (feat. Tell)
She Will by Lil Wayne (feat. Drake)
Ms. New Booty by Bubba Sparxxx (feat. Ying Yang Twins)
Slob on My Knob by Tear Da Club Up Thugs
Freaky Gurl by Gucci Mane (feat. Ludacris & Lil Kim)
Rich Sex (feat. Lil Wayne)
Tear da Club Up '97 by Three 6 Mafia
RNB by Young Dolph (feat. Megan Thee Stallion)
What about Your Friends by TLC

ONE

N 'Dea broke her own rule, "Never stay at the club alone." She went clubbing all the time with her girls. Their motto was, "We come together—we leave together." Tonight was different though. Her girls left already but she didn't want to end the night yet. It's barely 1:00 a.m., the nightclub was still lit, she wanted to keep partying (even if she was solo).

N'Dea was at the bar getting another drink. She leaned back against the bar to scan the club, while sipping her fruit flavored mixed drink. She's unaware of the eyes watching her. N'Dea bounced back out on the crowded dance floor. Her skin tight mini dress and sky high stilettos was limiting her to low level wiggling and twerking, Her movements were slower so it looked sexy. She was floating on cloud nine as the alcohol from her countless drinks starts taking over. She leaves the dance floor as the DJ starts playing a slow song. *Ugh-ain't nobody in love in here.*

"Where you going shorty?" A tall man with muscular arms leaned down to ask her.

"Do I know you?" N'Dea looked him up and down. She thought he was cute.

"I'm trying to get to know you. Let me get you another drink." He nods at her empty glass. "Whatchu drinking on?"

N'Dea is pleased he's willing to spend money. "Don't you wanna know?" She walks with slow deliberate steps to give him an eyeful on her way to the bar.

The cute guy with the arms is super close to N'Dea leaving no space between them. "Whatchu want?"

"Amaretto Sour, double shot."

He orders her drink along with his. "What's ya name shorty?"

"N'Dea."

"What's up N'Dea, I'm Trigger."

They get their drinks and continue the small talk over the next two-three songs. Trigger orders another round that N'Dea accepts with a smile. He's watching her with a sly smile. "What's up N'Dea, you wanna leave?"

Her words now slurred, "Nope. I'm good."

"I know you're good, shorty, let's go to my place." He places his hand on her waist, pulling her into him. She blushed, soaking up the attention. "My place is 10 minutes from here. It's quiet there." He was leaning down close to her ear, allowing his lips to graze her ear. She placed her hand on his chest to push away.

"No."

"What you mean no?" His voice elevating. "What you think I'm buying you all these drinks for? You know how this goes."

"I said NO."

He grabs her arm, "I don't take no for an answer. You feel me?"

N'Dea yanks her arm away. "You better get off—

"She said no." The stranger interrupted, positioning herself between N'Dea & Trigger. "My boyfriend is right over there." She pointed toward a man not far away. "You don't want this smoke."

Trigger rattled off insults before walking away.

"Are you ok, Sis?"

N'Dea replied, "Yeah. He was being a jerk."

"You looked like you could use some help."

"I appreciate it. I can't believe him—dudes be trippin."

"Don't they?" They laughed.

"He 'bout to kill my buzz." N'Dea frowned.

"Let me buy you a drink," the stranger offered. "I'm Shimmer." She smiled revealing a cute pair of dimples.

"What kind of name is Shim…Shimmer?"

"Excuse you rudeness?"

"My bad girl."

"What's your name rudeness?"

"N'Dea."

For the next twenty minutes or so, N'Dea and her new friend sat at the bar talking, laughing and drinking. Shimmer soaked up everything N'Dea said, leading her to believe they had a lot in common (soon they would).

"It's 'bout time for me to get outta here." N'Dea stood, unable to steady herself on the moving floor. She was sure the room was running laps around her. The flashing lights and smoke floating in the air didn't help.

"Are you gonna be alright to drive?" Shimmer offers her arm for balance.

N'Dea sits back down, leaning on the bar, placing her head in her hands. "I'm not driving, I rode with my friends. They left already so I gotta call a ride."

"Sounds like you need some new friends. Wanna come with me?"

N'Dea was tipsy but still felt uneasy about riding with the pretty stranger. "Can I trust you?"

Shimmer rolled her eyes. "You think I wanna do something to you? I'm trying to help you. You leaving with me or nah?"

TWO

Shimmer helps N'Dea get in her C300, "I need your address."

"Yeah, it's 123 Street. Ha Ha Ha Ha."

"Girl, you're tore up. Ha Ha Ha." Shimmer passes a bottle of water to N'Dea. "Take a sip, it'll help you sober up."

"Ew, your water tastes funny."

"Drink it."

N'Dea takes a huge gulp before passing the bottle back to Shimmer.

Shimmer sees N'Dea beginning to doze off.

"N'Dea."

"Huh?"

"Where do you stay at?"

"I told you. I live at the White House."

"Give me your license."

N'Dea passes her purse to Shimmer. She leans back in the seat, her eyes heavy from intoxication.

Shimmer shakes N'Dea's arm, "Unlock your cell phone so I can use your GPS."

N'Dea opens her bloodshot eyes and grabs her phone. "2552," she says aloud as she punches her code in.

"Now you can go to sleep." Shimmer smirks to herself while powering off the cellphone.

N'Dea is out cold. Her petite frame is no match for the powerful substances circulating in her bloodstream. She has no clue she's being double teamed by an undefeated opponent. The large quantity of alcohol she'd guzzled and the surprise Shimmer slipped to her, had her out for the count. Maybe she shouldn't wake up—if she knew what's waiting for her.

Shimmer is focusing on the road and her rearview mirror. She's watching the car that's been following her turn-for-turn for the past 15 minutes, damn near on her bumper. She is 20 minutes away from her destination. The car behind her jumps beside her. She can't see the driver of the Dodge Charger, the tent is too dark. The driver revs the engine releasing obnoxious noise, then speeds away. Shimmer rolls her eyes, "damn showoff," she mumbles. Sleeping beauty is none the wiser, but soon she would be.

Shimmer makes a few extra turns looking for the perfect location. BINGO! She spots a small church that sits back from the road. *There's no way they have cameras.* She goes into the trunk grabbing her survival kit. It contains wigs, ball caps, slides, sweatpants, hoodies, sunglasses and her overnight bag. Shimmer hurries to change, then does the same to her ride along. Shimmer threw their belongings in the overnight bag and put it in the trunk. She takes a black backpack out the trunk, tosses it on the passenger and peels out.

Shimmer is on cloud nine en route to their final destination (for the night). This part never gets old, she lives for the excitement. She considers herself an actress, cuz she's definitely playing a role. Her eyes identify the spot she's heading to.

Shimmer zips into the parking lot, driving around to the back, away from the cameras and lights. She backs into a space close to the door. There's no one in sight—perfect. She puts the girl's purse in the backpack and puts it on. Shimmer hops out and pulls her acquaintance out too. *Good thing she ain't that big, this would be impossible if she was a big bitch.* With one arm Shimmer balances N'Dea, she uses her other hand to place the key against the keypad. Shimmer hears the electronic lock release, she pushes open the door for them both. She hears the loud roaring of a super charged engine creeping into the lot.

Shimmer looks over her shoulder, catching a glance of the Dodge Charger, the showoff. She rushes into her hotel room. Shimmer dumps the girl on the second bed. It's a mess with clothes and wigs strewn about. She drops the backpack there too. Shimmer heads to the bathroom to empty her full bladder. She returns to the room wearing only her bra & panties, positioning herself on the bed closest to the door.

It's almost 4 a.m. Shimmer noticed as she lies back on the bed. *Damn, I put in work today.* She is happy with her accomplishment. Shimmer hears someone outside her door. She jumps up rushing to the door.

The door opens, "What's up baby?"

"Hey daddy."

Shimmer wrapped her arms around his neck, sharing her tongue with him.

"You missed me huh?"

"You know I did, daddy."

"She's still out?" He nods toward the passed out girl. "How much you gave her?"

"Uh Huh—don't blame me. I ain't give her that much. It's cuz her lil ass drank so much. She'll probably come to in a lil bit."

"You came in clutch tonight. I'm glad you peeped she was by herself."

"My eyes see everything. You like your present?" She points to the girl.

He nods up and down and starts undressing. "How long it's gonna take you to get her ready?"

Shimmer assures Trigger it's not gonna take long to get the new girl ready. He throws her on the empty bed, making her earn her stay as his main girl. Shimmer let him have his way, as usual, to keep him satisfied. New girls come and go, but she's been riding with Trigger for 2 years. They understood each other.

Trigger hopped in the shower once they finished having sex. He didn't let Shimmer join him so she could stay in the room and watch the girl. When he's done, Shimmer switches places with him.

Upon returning to the room, Shimmer sees Trigger looking over the girl. She recognizes the glimmer in his eyes as they travel up and down her body. He does this with every new girl. It reminds her of a kid on Christmas that can't wait to play with their new toy.

"She's little, huh?" Trigger asked.

Shimmer nods in agreement.

"She's already dressed the part. Once you get her right with hair, nails and lashes—he nods to himself, she's gonna be right."

"Yeah Daddy, we're gonna get that paper."

"Hell yeah."

"They won't know what hit 'em."

Trigger directs Shimmer to take care of the girl before they go to bed.

Shimmer follows Triggers's orders. She starts by stripping the girl naked. Next, she ties up her wrists and ankles. Shimmer uses a scarf to cover the girl's eyes.

"Naw don't use that," Trigger directs Shimmer. She puts the roll of duct tape down that she'd planned to put over the girl's mouth.

"What if she tries to scream?"

"Don't use that—she might throw up—that'll make her choke."

"Damn baby, you're right." Shimmer uses a scarf instead. They climb into bed with their captive secured in the bed next to them. Neither falls asleep right away.

Shimmer knew she'd be busy getting the newbie ready. The girl seemed green so her training might take awhile (but she wouldn't tell Trigger that). Her top goal was to make sure the girl understood how to play her position *behind* her.

Trigger is admiring their latest catch. She has potential. He hopes she can fall in line so he can keep her around for awhile. Shimmer may have brought home her replacement. He can't wait to welcome her to the family.

THREE

T rigger couldn't wait to get a sample. After a few hours he was awake, helping himself to the naked new girl. He could hear muffled moans she was making. *She's probably faking like she's still sleep. I bet her ass wake up.* He didn't know Shimmer was faking being asleep. She was watching him have his way with her competition, wishing it were her instead. Trigger continued ravishing his latest conquest. *I'll bring her ass back to life.*

N'Dea dreams she is floating—through the fog. Her vision is blurry. She hears muffled noises. There's pulling on her body and pounding on her head. Her throat is in desperate need of water. She sees the man doing push-ups, butt ass naked. His body is ripped. His shoulder blades flexing with each movement. All types of bulging muscles make up his massive arms. He increases his speed, and readjusts his tight waist and hips. That's when she sees the naked, motionless girl underneath him. Is he raping her? He readjusts again and she sees the girl's face. It's her own.

N'Dea wakes up to a man on top of her. She can hardly see or speak. *Why can't I see? What's in my mouth? How come I can't move my arms and legs?* She tries to wiggle side to side but can't move much either way.

Her movement arouses Trigger. He keeps drilling her, while sliding the scarf off her eyes. "What's up Shorty? Remember me?" She doesn't respond. "I told you I don't take no for an answer." He slows his rhythm down. "I'm going to take the rag out ya mouth, but if you try to scream or anything, I'll put a bullet in you." He grabs his handgun from his side and places it by her head. He pulls the scarf from her mouth. She remains silent. When he finishes, he grabs his gun, then removes her other restraints.

N'Dea sits up, pulling the blanket over her in an attempt to cover herself from the stranger. She notices a girl sleeping in the other bed. *What the hell is going on?*

"Peep game shorty. You belong to me now. You're my girl and work for me." She stared at him with glossed over eyes. He points to the girl on the bed, "That's Shimmer, she's gonna get you together." He explains how Shimmer will get her ready to work. Tears start flowing from her eyes.

"What's your name shorty?"

SILENCE

He picks up the handgun. N'dea clenches her eyes shut. Her body trembling from uncertainty. "Open your eyes." Trigger explains she doesn't have to be scared. "You'll be fine as long as you do what I say. You feel me?" She nods. "I asked you a question."

"N'Dea," she responded barely audible.

"You learn fast. Good for you shorty." Trigger tells her he's good to his girls. He takes care of them and they take care of him. He puts the heat back down.

"You will call me Daddy. You feel me?"

"Yes, Daddy."

"Smart girl. Shimmer, get up." The girl starts turning and

stretching, then opens her eyes and sits up. Shimmer's been up the whole time eavesdropping on their conversation.

"What should her new name be? I'm thinking Lady."

"Naw, that ain't it."

"How 'bout Lovely?"

"Hell no."

"What the hell Shimmer?"

"Oooh, I got it. Lacey." Shimmer walks over to Trigger. "What's up baby? I'm Shimmer and that's my girl Lacey. You wanna party?"

"Hell yeah. That's it," said Trigger.

Shimmer tongues him down, marking her territory. She smiles at N'Dea revealing deep set dimples. It clicks! The asshole with the arms. The girl with the dimples. The truth takes the wind outta her.

Shimmer picks up the heat, admiring it in her hand, then looks at N'Dea. Shimmer walks up to N'Dea with a huge smile on her face, showcasing her evil dimples. Shimmer's smile transitions to a dirty look as she points the gun squarely at N'Dea's head.

Shimmer tells N'Dea, "That man is mine. I'm his number 1, not you. If you don't do what he says or what I say, I'll fill your little ass with the whole clip. Understand?"

"Yes."

"Good," Shimmer hands the gun to Trigger. Without warning, Shimmer unloaded an early morning ass whooping on N'Dea. She delivered punches, kicks and elbows. N'Dea is caught off guard, still in a daze, and grappling with a hangover. She cowered under the stranger's assault. Shimmer grabbed a handful of N'Dea's hair trying to rip it from her scalp. She whispered, "You better not yell. Take it." The only thing N'Dea let out were silent tears.

"Alright Shimmer, y'all can play later. We need to go. Pack this shit up."

"OK Daddy," she released N'Dea's hair. "You heard Daddy,

start packing."

N'Dea did as she is told, realizing her life depended on it. A million thoughts traveling through her foggy mind.

Who are these people?

What do they want with me?

Where am I?

How did I get here?

The number one thought invading her mind—

How can I escape?

N'Dea hoped her mother and friends realized something was wrong. They had to be looking for her, right? She realized she had to play it cool until the right time presented itself for her to get away.

N'Dea was in the car with Shimmer as they headed west on I-20. "Me and you gonna spend a whole lotta time together so I can teach you the game. We'll be like sister wives or some shit." Shimmer was going over the tricks of the trade. "We work the clubs getting girls or simps, don't matter, as long as we make money for Daddy." Shimmer told N'Dea all the money goes to Trigger, in turn, he bankrolls their lifestyle. He pays for everything. "He's not bad to work for—he's better than most of the others."

"The others?"

"Damn Lacey, you can't be that green." Shimmer rolled her eyes. "You'll figure it out. Anyways, Daddy said we're going shopping to get you some sexy shit to take pics in. We gotta get you out there. We're 'bout to get this paper."

N'Dea pushed down the anxiety rising in her. Shimmer thought she was hyping her up but it was having the opposite effect. N'Dea is terrified, holding back tears as a lump formed in her throat.

Shimmer damn near sent N'Dea into a full-blown panic attack with her next statement. "Daddy's gonna put you to work soon."

FOUR

What's up with all these tricks wanting to be called *Daddy?* N'Dea thought as the trick pounded her. "Oh yeah, that's it Daddy," Lacey encouraged him. It was either "call me daddy" or "tell me it's mine." She'd lost count of the number of tricks she'd serviced since Daddy put her to work days after Shimmer said he would. The trick finished and left, leaving her alone on the bed.

Trigger came back, "Aye baby, you got 'bout 30 minutes before ya next one. I'm trying to find a walk-in to squeeze in there cuz I know you like getting this money for Daddy."

"That's right Daddy, anything for you."

"My favorite girl got 5 minutes for me?" He comes to the bed. "Top me off real quick—sloppy." N'Dea spits on it and goes to work. It doesn't take him long to explode in her mouth.

"Swallow that shit for Daddy."

"Mmmm, you taste so good." She bites her lower lip.

"You better do it just like that for the tricks too, keep 'em coming back."

"I do Daddy, just like you told me, whatever they want."

"You better cuz if you don't—they're gonna snitch and then Daddy has to punish you. Remember last time?"

"That don't happen no more. I do what I gotta do to get Daddy's money."

"That's why you're my favorite." I'ma go check on your sister. He left for Shimmer's room.

This was N'Dea's life now: tricking, lying, crying, and most of all dying. Everything she had now: the wigs, clothes, shoes, the fake name & age…all belonged to Trigger—even her life. Everything she did catered to Trigger, Shimmer and the tricks.

There was no evidence of who she used to be. Her social media accounts were closed after she made a handful of posts. Trigger stood out of camera view with his heat pointed at her while she went live. This tactic intended to trick her Mom, friends and police into believing she was fine and left on her own. She'd give anything to have her old life back.

Trigger opens the door for her next customer, snapping her back to her present life. She takes a double shot of erk & jerk to the head. "Hey baby, I'm Lacey." She rolls onto her knees, arches her back and looks over her shoulder. She licks her lips. "I've been waiting for you. You wanna come play with me?"

CHAPTER
FIVE

T rigger spent 2 months taking his business all over metro Atlanta. They were criss-crossing from Gwinnett and Cobb to Clay Co, DeKalb and Fulton counties. They fled down 75 south and settled in a college town. Lacey would fit in well here. She was a key addition to his family. She pulled in all types of clients who payed top dollar for her because she looked so young. Who wouldn't wanna party with her?

Lacey is in her element in the south Georgia club, sipping on Hennessy—no chaser. The Albany club is packed, full of locals and college kids. Every club was the same, full of the usual characters with a role to play. Every club wants to be full of baddies, dimes…eye candy. They attract the other characters. The women are on the prowl for the hustlers, their next sponsor to come up. The hustlers hunt the eye candy, looking for their next wifey, side chick or fling.

The baddies & hustlers are easy to spot. The other characters, the pretenders, operate in the background. Their true intent deceptive. They're lurking until they catch another character slippin.

Lacey made her way to the dance floor. The loud music vibrating through her small frame. She bopped to three songs, before returning to the bar. With her liquid courage in her hand, she makes her way to the opposite end of the bar. She stands near a handsome man with bulging biceps. The music is too loud to hear the conversation he's having with the beautiful young woman, so she watches them, waiting for the cue.

"Aye man, let her go."

"Who the hell are you?" The man asks.

"Don't worry about who the hell I am. My man over there knows who I am. Try me if you want and he'll light this whole club up to take ya ass out."

The stranger drops the young woman's arm. "I don't need this shit, you ain't that fine anyway." He walks away.

"Are you ok?"

"Yeah. He was mad cuz I ain't wanna leave with him."

"You looked like you could use some help."

"Thanks, weak ass men can't take no for an answer."

"Girl, I know. You don't gotta tell me." They laughed.

"Don't let his lame ass ruin your night. Let me buy you a drink. I'm Lacey." She smiled.

"Thanks. I'm Pageant."

"You do beauty pageants or some shit?"

"Yeah, I used to and so did my mom."

"That's dope," said Lacey. "Girl, this end of the bar is moving too slow. I'ma go down to the other end. You ain't gonna dip the minute I walk away are you?"

"Naw, I wouldn't do that since you had my back."

"What you drinking on, Pageant?"

"Surprise me."

"I got you," Lacey smiles before disappearing.

At the other end of the bar, Lacey finishes her drink, then orders a round of doubles for her and Pageant. She hands Pageant's drink to Shimmer with a subtle nod. "Carry this one."

Lacey rejoins Pageant. Lacey introduces Shimmer to Pageant.

"Pageant, this is my cousin Shimmer."

"Hey, here's your drink." Shimmer passes the drink to Pageant. Her and Lacey glancing at each other as Pageant sips the drink.

"So Pageant, how you know my cousin?"

"I don't. She jumped in when this asshole was being too pushy." She gulps the alcohol.

"I had to check, she's so friendly. I gotta look out for her. You might be crazy." Shimmer looks Pageant up and down.

"I ain't crazy."

"I told her she looks familiar. I think I've seen you around campus," Lacey lies.

"Yeah, you probably did."

"Oh, so y'all both go to school. Let me get another round of drinks. I'll be back." Shimmer heads back to the far end of the bar. Lacey and Pageant continue their conversation until Shimmer returns with their drinks. The three ladies keep talking, laughing and drinking. Lacey hangs on to everything Pageant says. She continues to deceive her so she'll believe they're both students at the university.

"You need a ride back to campus?" Lacey asks Pageant.

"Yeah, my girls left already cuz they work in the morning."

"Oh, so you're a party girl," Lacey said.

"Sounds like you need some new friends." Shimmer tells her. "I guess you can ride with us since you know my cousin. You ain't gonna try nothing crazy are you?"

"Who me? You can trust me. Can I trust y'all?" Pageant asked.

Lacey rolled her eyes. "What you think we're gonna do? We're trying to help a sista out—a fellow ram. You coming?"

Pageant weighs her options. *Leave with the girls now. Get a free ride—they offered. Be relaxed if I ride with other women. Find someone to bum a ride with. Wait til they're ready to go. Pay for a ride to come. Leave with a guy means gotta keep my guard up.*

Several party-goers start departing. Shimmer is among them to bring the car up. Everyone is on their way somewhere different. Some are headed to the next party. Others will grab some late night Waffle House. Many will find a bedroom, theirs or someone else's, to occupy until the morning.

Pageant makes her decision. "Thanks girl, but I don't—

"When you break your own rules, you live by someone else's."
THE END.

Potential ending 1:

"Thanks girl, but I don't—I don't wanna bother you anymore. I'm good. I'll wait for my homeboy."

Potential ending 2:

"Thanks girl, but I don't—I don't know what I would've done if I didn't meet up with y'all. 'Preciate it cuz I don't feel like waiting for a ride."

Which ending did Pageant choose? Stay tuned to find out.

Thanks for reading! You're now a #EQReader. Please help me out and leave a review on Amazon. Include the hashtag in your review.

REVIEWS

I'd love to hear your comments and thoughts on this story. Please leave a review or send me a message.

Go to https://www.authorebonyq.com/contact

SEEK HELP

IF YOU OR SOMEONE YOU KNOW IS AFFECTED BY DOMESTIC VIOLENCE OR RELATIONSHIP ABUSE, HELP IS AVAILABLE.

NATIONAL DOMESTIC VIOLENCE HOTLINE
WEBSITE: https://www.thehotline.org
CALL: 800-799-7233
TEXT: "START" TO 88788

IF YOU ARE A VICTIM OF HUMMAN TRAFFICKING, GET HELP.

NATIONAL HUMAN TRAFFICKING HOTLINE
WEBSITE: www.TraffickingResourceCenter.org
CALL: 1-888-3737-888
TEXT: "HELP" TO 233733 (BE FREE)

EXCLUSIVES

Sign-up for my email list to receive Ebony Q. Exclusives. Be the first to find out what I'm working on. I won't spam you or share your info. You can unsubscribe at anytime.

Join my journey here: https://www.authorebonyq.com

Want to keep the story going? Get behind the scenes story info, like story inspiration.

Get more info at https://www.authorebonyq.com/blog

DISCUSSION/REFLECTION QUESTIONS

USE FOR A BOOK CLUB OR REFLECTION

1. What was your favorite or least favorite part of the book?
2. Which scene has stuck with you the most?
3. Did you reading the book impact your mood? If yes, how so?
4. What surprised you most about the book?
5. Did the book's title match the book's contents? If you could give the book a new title, what would it be?
6. Are there lingering questions from the book you're still thinking about?
7. Did the book strike you as original?
8. How did the author keep you interested or surprised throughout the story?
9. Are there any characters you wish you could have given advice to? What would you tell them?
10. Did this book seem realistic?
11. Did the characters seem believable to you? Did they remind you of anyone?
12. How relevant or relatable are the themes or messages of the book to your own life, or to society today?

13. How did you feel about the ending? Was it satisfying or did you want more?
14. What do you think happens to the characters after the novel concludes? What do you think Pageant decides to do?
15. Would you want to read read another book by this author?

Authors enjoy hearing from their readers. Share your response to one of these questions with the author.

Go to https://www.authorebonyq.com/contact

ALSO BY EBONY Q.

Meet Majesty & Elegance, two sisters who disagree on how Elegance raises her troubled son Divine. Majesty knows her nephew Divine is bad as hell. She can't understand why his mother doesn't think so. Elegance believes she must protect her son since everyone else is against him... especially her sister Majesty.

The family faces a crisis when Divine does the unthinkable. What will it cost them? Everything.

See the book trailer at www.authorebonyq.com

Get your copy at Amazon.com/author/ebonyq or Barnes & Noble

COMING SOON

DISILLUSIONED: A TWISTED LOVE STORY

I wake up in bed alone. Where's Brentay? He always comes home, even if it's late. I'll call him in a minute. I get ready for work so I won't be late. I need the hours. We need the money.

It's getting harder and harder for me to keep working all these extra hours. I wish I could call in but I can hear Brent saying, "Being tired is an excuse for being lazy, so get it or don't." It's one of his many sayings. I'm dressed and ready to go. I need to make some coffee and dash out the door.

I open our bedroom door and almost faint. My mouth drops open. I stop in my tracks, clutching my chest. Why is Brentay asleep with three half naked women all over him?

I scan the normally tidy living room. It's a mess.

Empty glasses.

Liquor bottles.

Women's clothing.

Stiletto heels.

Are these girls stripers?

And why does it smell like weed in here?

Oh I don't believe this. My man is in his drawers with not

one, not two, but THREE women in *my* house. How could he bring this filth to *our* home?

Now it's *my* turn to have an episode. I go to the kitchen like I planned. I grab a butcher's knife from the drawer and go back to the living room. *I could gut them all now....*

GET DISILLUSIONED... JANUARY 2024

BONUS CONTENT 1
CHARACTER TALKS: LACEY

Character Introduction

Author Ebony Q: I'm excited and a little nervous for today's interview. I have the privilege of having Lacey here. She's the main character in my story Party Girl. Thank you for agreeing to the interview.

Lacey: (Nods) MmmHmm

Author Ebony Q: Let me notify the readers that we will only identify today's guest by Lacey and no other name.

Lacey: Right cuz that is my name so…

Author Ebony Q: Understood. Also, I want the readers to know Lacey is accompanied by a male companion, who will remain unnamed.

Lacey: That's my friend/bodyguard.

Author Ebony Q: Bodyguard? Do you need protection from someone?

Lacey: (rolls eyes) Yes, cuz it's a lot of crazies out there. My friend protects me…makes sure I'm good. Next question.

The Real Story

Author Ebony Q: It seems like you were *held* against your will, were you?

Lacey: No

Unidentified male: Things ain't always how they seem.

Author Ebony Q: I think the readers would agree with you. Were you *taken* against your will?

Unidentified male: She said no. Move on.

Author Ebony Q: Were you drugged or given something you weren't aware of?

Lacey: No. I see what you're trying to do. Let me say, that first night in the club, my girls shouldn't have left me. We had a rule in place for a reason.

Author Ebony Q: What reason is that?

Lacey: I already told you it's a lot of crazies out there.

Author Ebony Q: Did you meet some crazy people that night?

Lacey: No. I met some friends who helped me.

We Have To Know

Tell the Truth

Keep it Real

Author Ebony Q: The readers want to know why didn't you try to escape?

Lacey: Escape? You sound crazy. Escape from what? Ain't nothing to escape from.

Author Ebony Q: Are you in danger?

Unidentified male: This is over. Let's go.

Author Ebony Q: Where's Shimmer? What happened with Pageant?

Lacey: You tried it. Let your readers know I'm good.

My Final Thoughts

Let's wrap-up

The interview ended abruptly after I asked if Lacey was in danger. Her answers seemed very rehearsed, controlled by her male companion. She isn't ready yet to tell the truth—I'm not sure she knows what the truth is...anymore. Stay safe Lacey.

Keep the Party Going with Trigger's interview coming up next.

BONUS CONTENT 2
CHARACTER TALKS: TRIGGER

Character Introduction

Author Ebony Q: I have mixed feelings for today's interview with Trigger. He's the leading man in my story Party Girl. Thank you for agreeing to talk to me.

Trigger: I'm here—don't got nothing to hide. You know you can call me Daddy, if you want.

Author Ebony Q: I'm not calling you that. Nothing to hide… what's your real name?

Trigger: Don't play with me. What was my name in the story? That's my name. Move on.

The Real Story

Let's go deeper…

Author Ebony Q: Do you admit you pimp women?

Trigger: Pimp? No. I'm a protector. A provider.

Author Ebony Q: Don't the women really provide for you? They work for you, right?

Trigger: Yes, I'm a promoter.

Author Ebony Q: What do you promote? Prostitution?

Trigger: Hell No. I ain't no criminal. Did my time—ain't going back. I promote a good time. I run a dating service.

Author Ebony Q: A dating service?

Trigger: A lot of men want female companionship. We offer that.

Author Ebony Q: Do the women have a choice in any of this?

Trigger: Hell yeah, they always have a choice. With every choice there's a consequence. They understand that.

We Have To Know

Tell the Truth

Keep it Real

Author Ebony Q: Do you love your women? Shimmer? Lacey?

Trigger: I love…how good I am to my business partners. We work well together.

Author Ebony Q: Is it love when you rape, drug, kidnap and force the women, "your partners," to be sex workers?

Trigger: I don't know what you talking' 'bout with all that. Really though, what is love? Who loves me? Not these women? Women don't love nobody. My mama taught me that.

Author Ebony Q: What's up with your Mother? Do y'all have a relationship?

Trigger: The only relationship that matters to me is getting paid. That lady don't care about me & I don't give a damn about her.

Author Ebony Q: You don't have love for anyone? Shimmer seems to love you.

Trigger: Shimmer loves the life I give her, the life I rescued her from. I got love for my uncle.

Author Ebony Q: What does your uncle think about your line of work?

Trigger: He's the one that put me on—realest man I know.

Author Ebony Q: What is one thing readers should know about you?

Trigger: Women want a man to take control and take care of them. That's what I do. I'm a good guy, ask Shimmer.

Author Ebony Q: Oh, I will.

Trigger: If you ever want a different life, full of fun…holla at ya boy.

Author Ebony Q: You can't be serious. That ends this interview. Thanks (I guess) for talking to the readers.

Trigger: Anything for you, my favorite girl. Anything.

My Final Thoughts

Let's wrap-up

Trigger believes his own lies. Do you think his "business partners" know the real him? Definitely need to dig to find out more about his mother. I feel like I need a shirt that says #Free Shimmer & #Free Lacey.

PARTY GIRL 2 (INTRO)
THE PREQUEL: INNOCENCE LOST

Welcome to the origin story of Shimmer and Trigger. Peek into their past to uncover their family background. Learn what led them to be who they are. Uncover what factors caused their choices in Party Girl.

Ready to go deeper with the people you've learned to love... or love to hate? See how innocence is lost in Party Girl 2, the prequel. The question is, whose innocence is lost, theirs or yours?

WARNING... It's about to get spicy!

STOP here if you can't handle the heat.

If you like it hot... Spread my pages.

PARTY GIRL 2 (CHAPTER 1)
THE PREQUEL: INNOCENCE LOST

Sage devours all the attention he is giving her. He's spitting game and she's down to play. Their flirting started two weeks ago when they met. It's Friday—her first night—he's busy welcoming her to the spot.

"Shawty, you bad." Brick licks his lips.

"I know," Sage agrees, "you better recognize."

Brick pressed himself against Sage, backing her into the desk in the office. "I wanna do more than recognize."

Sage arches her back against the desk. The citrus and woodsy smell of his cologne was sending her hormones in overdrive. "What you wanna do?"

He looks down on her. "You."

He kisses her gently on her neck. "I wanna taste." He licks her neck leaving it wet.

Sage smiles, unknowingly revealing her youth and inexperience to the older, more experienced predator. Brick pulls her shirt up, freeing her young, perky breasts. He covers them in sloppy kisses. His hand travels down south, grabbing her womanhood. Brick jams his fingers in her.

"Ugh - Ow baby. Not so rough."

"Shut-up and take it." He returns his mouth back to her breasts. He slurps them up, then begins biting.

Is he biting my titties?

"It feels good, right? You like it?"

"Yeah, I like it." Sage lied, trying to focus on the pleasure instead of the pain.

Brick's erection is full grown and ready to poke something. He drops his baggy pants & boxers to free his third leg. Brick pulls down her booty shorts and thrusts himself deep inside her.

Sage wonders if this is what her mother meant when she said, "Nothing good will come out of you following your sister to that club." *She's old, what does she know? If this is what I gotta do to make it to the top, I'm with it.*

"Turn that ass around." Brick slides out of her. Sage turns around, pressing her stomach against the desk. Brick grips her ass then attempts to enter it.

"Ow - Ow baby." Sage tensed and held her muscles. "I never did—

"I thought you were grown. I'll go get another trick to party with."

"I'm down baby, I wanna party with you. It just hurts." Sage let out.

Brick waddles around to the front of the desk with his jeans and drawers around his ankles. He opened the bottom drawer and pulls out a paper bag. He opens the bottle of brown liquor inside the bag. He drinks from the bottle before passing it to Sage. She begins guzzling, feeling the burn in the back of her throat. Brick sits on the couch, enjoying the show. He starts running his hand up & down his pole, not wanting to lose his erection.

"Bring your sexy ass over here." He increases his hand speed. "Give me some drank."

Sage passes him the bottle.

"Come taste this." Brick directs her to get on her knees.

Sage begins her mouth work. *He's big big.*

Brick looks down at the trick in training as her head is bobbing up and down. He loves the fringe benefits of helping out in the club. The young ones are so eager to make a name for themselves, they'll do anything. It was time to get what he really wanted.

"Watch out" Brick pushes her shoulders back so she could release him. "I wanna see that ass clap."

She bites her lower lip as she slides off his lollipop. "What, you want me to dance?"

"Hell no, I'll see that in a minute. Stay on your knees. He pushes her up against the couch. Sage feels the moisture left behind from his sweat. It smells good like his cologne. Brick passes her the liquor. "Drink some more."

Again she took the bottle to the head.

"Now relax. I got you." Brick slaps her ass.

Sage felt wetness all over her ass cheeks as the liquor ran down her. He uses one hand to spread her cheeks open and uses the other hand to pour brown liquor down her ass crack. He massages her ass. "I got you." He plays with the liquor on her ass. "I'ma just put the head in, ok?"

"OKKKKKKKKKKKK," Sage screams as she felt his head and every inch of his long, thick manhood enter her back door.

"You're doing good. Just relax," Brick coaches her. He begins moving in and out of her in a slow pace to get her used to it. "Damn baby, this ass is tight."

Sage didn't answer because she is biting the cushions. Sage planned to pop P tonight, but only on the stage. This was new to her. She did doggy-style before but not this. She didn't like it, but since he did, she would learn to love it.

49

"Give me this ass girl." Brick grips her ass cheeks and continues her orientation. Brick knew he had to tag her first. *As pretty & dumb as she is, it won't take anytime before the club turns her ass out. At least I hit first.*

Sage hopes he'll hurry up and finish. It feels like he is stretching her insides out.

—It hurt.

—It burns.

—It is awful.

She keeps her face buried in the couch cushions, her jaws clenched tight. This hurt worse than when she got her cherry popped when she was in 8th grade.

Brick slid out of her yams and slid into her wet walls, this time without any resistance. He caught his rhythm and begins pounding the hell outta her. Where he was gentle before, he is savage now. *Ain't no way anybody ever hit it like this.* Her ass was jiggling all over the place. "You 'bout to be my #1 girl if you give it to me like this all the time."

Sage likes the sound of that. He damn near proposed to her. *Mrs. Sage... Note to self: I gotta find out his last name... and his real name. Anyways, when Brick takes over the club I'll be right by his side, just like he promised. Mama won't be the only one married to a man with money.*

"You ready girl?" He grunted while gripping her ass like a vice grip.

"Yeah," she moaned.

"Here I come."

Sage felt the warm fluid splatter against the small of her back & her ass as Brick shoots his load on her.

"I'ma need some more of this later." Brick got up and fixed his clothes. "Hurry up so you can go to the back and get ready, it's almost midnight. Let me school you real quick about this place. A lot of the girls gonna hate on you, you're younger, prettier, and ya fat ass is real."

"Facts." Sage blushed at the compliments revealing her deep set dimples.

"To keep the hate low, don't let them know you're my girl. Ya feel me? Keep this between us."

"What?"

"If they know you're mine, them hoes gonna try to throw ass at me to piss you off. It's better if they don't know."

Sage couldn't hide the disappointment spreading across her face. He caught her off guard.

"I don't wanna be your sneaky link."

"You're not but we don't need everybody in our business. Trust me baby girl."

Sage nods in agreement. *I'll do it for now.*

"I'm here to make sure you're good. That's why I wanted to break you off." He patted his crotch. "To make you feel good and have you relax." Brick told Sage how a lot of girls are nervous on their first night. He told her to hit the bottle right before she comes out & when she hits the stage to look for him. "I got you." He winks at her.

"I ain't scared, I'm ready." Sage cleans herself and put her clothes back on.

"Slow down Shawty, it's rough out there." Brick rubs his goatee.

"I like it rough." Sage licks her lips.

Brick nods, "Oh yeah, I know." *I know ya young ass don't have a clue but you're gonna fuck around and find out.*

Sage smiles.

She got the job she wanted.

She got her new man—a real one, the biggest boss.

Soon she'd have all eyes on her.

I'm 'bout to shine on 'em. They ain't ready for Shimmer. I'm already proving my mama wrong.

Things are moving fast.

It's either…

Her come up.

Or…

Her downfall.

PARTY GIRL 2
(CHAPTER 2)

THE PREQUEL: INNOCENCE LOST

Anise wants them to shut the hell up. She was over their tired conversation—messing up her Friday night. For twenty minutes, her girls were talking her ear off. The many conversations, in the crowded room, was subtle background noise compared to them. Even the loud music blaring from the speakers is being drowned out by these two nagging voices.

"I can't believe you're gonna let her do it?"

"Ain't no way I would."

"Don't be mad when she starts taking your shine."

"Right, bye bye Sparkle."

Anise couldn't take it anymore. "Damn, don't nobody wanna hear what y'all talkin' 'bout."

"We just tryin' to—

"Tryin' to what? Clearly, not mind your business. Try that." Anise interrupts and rolls her eyes. They were striking a nerve, hitting on some things she wasn't ready to face yet, but Anise would never admit it.

Anise did try to stop her. It didn't work...it never did. *Not my problem.* She thinks to herself. *I ain't no baby sitter. I gotta live my life. Let her momma ' n them worry about that.*

"Where the drinks at?" Anise asked.

"Oh, now you wanna chill with us?" Her friend jokes before passing her a red solo cup.

"Right, I wanna chill—not hear that noise y'all were bumping ya gums about."

Her other friend pulls a bottle of hen dog out of her oversized-bag. The three friends began their routine of drinking, doing their hair & make-up and spilling the tea.

"Angel, tell Anise who sent you a DM."

"Lower your damn voice." Angel spat while glancing around the room.

Lola rolled her eyes. "Why? Am I supposed to be scared?"

"I don't wanna have to go to jail tonight behind your big mouth."

"Who sent the dick message?" Anise leans in.

"My baby daddy don't play about me," Lola mocks their shared enemy.

Angel winks to confirm. "Girl, he sent dick pics and everything."

"And?" Anise probes her friend to tell her the whole story.

"And nothing," Angel lied.

"Oh, I know you did more than nothing with his fine paid ass."

"You already know," Lola chimes in. They all share a laugh.

"I can't wait for her dumbass to find out," Lola said. "Then she won't be walking around here like she better than everybody else."

"She ain't gonna find out," Angel wasn't revealing she has been sleeping around with Stoni's baby daddy for months now. She let her girls believe she'd just started bedding him down. He kept her paid and she kept their secret. Angel was a master at keeping secrets, like a priest in a confessional booth. Her livelihood depended on it.

"Stoni knows his ass ain't loyal," Anise adds. "He's only loyal to the streets."

"Lola c'mon and hook my hair up," Anise said.

"I got you boo," Lola loves doing hair.

"Lay my edges and give me a ponytail up top and long waves hanging down in the back," Anise instructed.

Lola starts gathering Anise's hair in a ponytail. "Oh, I forgot to tell y'all about my latest sponsor. He's old as hell."

"You're gonna mess around and get worms sleeping with them old men," Anise jokes.

Angel smiles and nods in agreement.

Lola continues telling her girls about her latest "sponsor." He works in finance and loves spending money on me. She tells them how she doesn't have to do much to get his money. "Y'all need to get you an old-head."

"Nope, I'm good." Anise frowns at the idea of sleeping with someone her father's age. She could never.

"I'm with Anise. I prefer the young guns," Angel says.

"The old heads are papered up," Lola said.

"Girl, you sexing somebody granddaddy." Anise frowns again.

"I'm sexing the granddaddy, daddy, uncle and whoever else throwing dollars," Lola smiles.

"We know," Angel smirks.

"I know you ain't talking cuz the only thing angel-like about you is your name. You're doing the same thing—you just keep yours on the down low." Lola reads Angel.

"Miss me with the I'm a virgin contest between y'all cuz both of y'all thots are way past that," Anise said.

"We learned from the Queen thot." Lola flicks her long tongue.

"MmmHmm, you're just like us so stop the cap," Angel backs up Lola.

Anise knew Angel wasn't trying to be slick but her statement had Anise tight. She promised herself she wouldn't follow that pathway. She didn't sleep with men for money. That wasn't the vibe.

"Are you done yet?" Anise was getting impatient.

"You can't rush perfection," Lola rolls her finger. "Unless you wanna look busted."

"Hurry the hell up so I can fix ya faces," Anise said.

Lola rolls her eyes and continues working on her friend's wig. The smell of burnt hair & hairspray seeps into the air. Several girls in the room were also in makeshift salon chairs getting their hair done. Everyone wanted a chance to sit in Lola's chair but she was very selective in this part of her life. It was easier to get in her pants than get in her chair.

The girls switch places and now Lola is seated while Anise glams her face. Anise loves doing Lola's make-up because she let her do whatever she wanted. Lola could rock any look and it always slays. Anise gave her an ultra glam look with a super bold lip. Lola loved drawing attention to her mouth and her long tongue. Anise hooks Angel up with a no make-up look with bold smokey eyes. Angel preferred a subtle make-up look. For herself, Anise did a soft glam look with glitter on her eyes to highlight the cat-eye. She finishes with nude, extra glossy lips.

The night was about to ramp up in more ways than one.

"Y'all cute."

None of them respond to the hater who was now invading their space.

"Y'all look almost as good as me...almost." Stoni smiles before sashaying away.

"I hate that bitch," Lola spat.

"I hate whoever gave her that lopsided fake ass," Anise follows Stoni with her eyes as she walks away.

"Don't worry about her. She'll get what's coming to her— trust," Angel said.

"Sis you're stupid. She got a BBL and the L stands for lopsided." Lola cracks up laughing. Her giggling is contagious. Her friends howl in laughter.

"No-No the L stands for low-rider." Angel grips her sides in hysterics.

They burst out laughing again. The girls calm down and finish off the alcohol. They are feeling good, the liquor erasing their issues from their mind, even if only temporary.

Anise's freedom runs away quicker than a New York minute as Brick walks in with a new girl. They yank Anise's attention to them. Brick was the owner's shady nephew. He tried to holla at all the new girls cuz the old heads knew better, ignoring his weak ass game. The new girl was cheesing hard, no doubt buying all the lies he is selling. Poor girl had no clue. Damn!

Anise is struggling with the tug-o-war pulling her back and forth. She wants to say, "My name is Ben-it and I ain't in it." But then Anise wants to help her. *I can try-TRY-to keep an eye on her, ya know, put her up on game. Hell, somebody needs to warn her with the quickness to stay away from Brick.* Anise is trying to convince herself there is nothing to worry about. *Don't lie to yourself. You know that's not true.* If "I'm down for whatever was a person," it's her, Queen of schemes.

Why'd she have to bring her ass in here?

Wherever Sage is her partner in crime, bullshit, rides shotgun.

THAT'S IT FOR NOW. STAY TUNED FOR THE FULL STORY.

About the Author

Ebony lives in Georgia. She has always loved to read urban fiction. She also enjoys watching true crime dramas. Ebony prides herself on writing fiction where real people, not characters, experience real-life situations. Her motto is, *"Telling our stories my way."*

Augusta, Ga riverwalk (Photo credit: Divine Gibbs)

Please tag me in a social media post showing the book cover & quote your favorite line or share your thoughts. Use the hashtags #EQReader and #authorebonyq.

Made in the USA
Columbia, SC
31 July 2024